Agreements and Curses

Johannes T. Evans

A young man is dispatched to a fae land and joins the princes' retinue.

20k, rated M, M/M. As part of an exchange program between the magical city from which he hails and the fae island state of Einsamal, a young man is sent as a child to explore fable and adventure, and in the process falls in love with one of the princes. The prince, a child of Loki, faces his own trials.

Some slow fantasy, a bit of romance and Norse trouble and emotions and angst. Introducing Princes Loptr and Fenris, Boniface Nottingham, aaaand with some more of Loki at his usual mischief.

Agreements and Curses

Boniface had spent much of the journey from Virtue lying on his side in the small berth that had been assigned him — only three times over the course of the three-week journey had he actually managed to get himself to his feet and get out on deck, and while the sea breeze would soothe him for a little while, it would be a short-lived relief before the sea sickness gripped him again.

When he alighted on Einsamal, it was a member of the king's court, a healer named Is, who came to meet him. He was fairly sure he looked awful already, but her look of horror made him quite certain.

"I'm sorry," he muttered as he followed after her, slow and a little clumsy on his feet. "They kept saying I'd get used to it, but I just... didn't."

"Sit," said Is, bringing him to sit down at a table and bench overlooking the port, and Boniface looked out to the ship as the crew kept climbing off of it — they'd bound the sails down, tied them up, and now they were passing cargo down the gangplank. The rest of it. The cargo that wasn't Boniface himself.

Is disappeared but returned with a plate of smoked meats, cheese, and a thick, grainy bread, and he ate ravenously — he was hungrier than he'd ever been in his life, unbelievably relieved to actually be able to chew and swallow without immediately gagging or feeling dizzy, and he knew it was impolite, that he should have been talking, but he was *starved*.

He'd met Is a few months ago, when Boniface's name had been drawn from the lottery, at least, so it wasn't as if she was a complete stranger.

"How was the ceremony?" she asked.

"Good," said Boniface. "She seems nice, Kari. She seemed tremendously... refined."

"It's part of the agreement that we exchange children of roughly equal value to our communities, that they might serve appropriate roles as they change places, assuming they grow into the community, stay there."

"She seemed like a princess," said Boniface, and Is laughed, shaking her head.

"She isn't a princess," she said. "But Kari is of noble birth — her mother is a commander in Einsamal's navy, and her father serves alongside myself, in his majesty's court."

"And that's equivalent to a cardiothoracic surgeon and the Head of the Treasury?"

"It was argued," said Is, "that Virtue might think we were cheating them, sending Kari instead of someone in line for the throne."

Boniface looked down at the surface of the table, feeling his cheeks burn. He didn't like it, being told how valuable he was based on what his parents did — and he absolutely didn't like being told how valuable someone else was, that they were less valuable than him. It felt wrong, felt unpleasant and almost dirty, somehow. He knew that it wasn't like that, exactly — he'd been given a very stern talking-to about it, that it was about value to the community rather than a monetary worth or something similar, but something about it didn't taste right to him, didn't sit well.

"Lady Astrid and Amund are sailing at the moment," said Is. "They'll be back before dark — you'll be raised in their household, under their purview, as Kari is being raised in yours. You understand?"

"Yes," said Boniface. "I'm very grateful, of course."

"Have you eaten your fill?"

"Yes, thank you."

"Then we'll walk up the hill," said Is. "You'll meet his majesty now, and his sons."

Boniface felt the blood drain out of his face, his stomach doing a flip, and he looked down at himself in his battered trousers and corded jumper, thought about the glimpse he'd got of his reflection, the mussed and dirty state of his hair, the bags under his eyes, how pale he was, how *unwell* he looked.

"Are you sure?" he asked.

"It's why I came to meet you," said Is. "You are to act as a noble's son — the princes are your peers now, Boniface."

"*Princes*," repeated Boniface helplessly.

"Come," said Is.

He was still clumsy walking up the hill, and he felt out of place in the clothes he was wearing — he'd been told his clothes would be alright, but he didn't see anybody else wearing clothes like his, clothes that you'd buy in shops with zips on them: everyone was wearing handmade pieces, many of them wearing tunics with layers of fabric and shawls rather than actual jumpers. He didn't see so much as a pair of jeans — the closest he saw were leather breeches, and that was some man going by on horseback.

People were looking at him, and he forced himself to keep his head high and to smile at the people that looked his way, to nod to them, even though he almost wanted to grab at Is' skirts and hide in them as though he were six instead of twelve.

The palace was sprawling and beautifully designed, but it was set inside the mountain, such that at first you thought you were just going into tunnels, and then you saw the incredible stained glass rooves and windows, letting in light that was turned a hundred beautiful colours by the designs in the glass and left to dapple on the floor.

They were walking on rainbows as they moved further into palace, and Boniface could feel his heart beating hard in his chest as they walked through and then past a room with a great throne in it, instead going out under the open air again. It was a small arena, dirt ground encircled with stone fencing, and Boniface stared at the boys sparring inside it.

They were about his own age, twelve or thirteen, but all three of them were bigger than he was, and stacked with muscle — the largest of them, an East Asian boy with thick brown hair tied up in a bun, moved astonishingly fast for a boy with such brawn on his body, and the two white ones, who were both big but lacked the same bulk their friend sported, were struggling to keep up with him, but made up for being a little slower by working together to try to trip him to the ground.

Looking out over them was a big, bulky man who resembled the biggest boy — he was over six feet tall, taller than Boniface's own father, and he was nodding slowly as he watched the boys fight.

When he turned his head and saw Boniface, his expression of focused concentration faded to a grinning smile, and he clapped a mighty hand down on Boniface's shoulder, winding him.

"There you are!" he said, and then frowned slightly, tilting up Boniface's face. "Fuck," he pronounced, making him blink a few times in surprise — he didn't think anyone had ever sworn so obviously in front of him, to him. "Had a hard time on the journey here, did ya?"

"It turns out I get seasick, your majesty," said Boniface, and King Leon laughed.

"We'll cure you of that, soon enough," he pronounced loudly. "Boniface Nottingham, Man of Virtue, well-met!"

He put out his arm, bending slightly so that Boniface could reach, and Boniface straightened his back, gripping the older man's forearm the way he gripped Boniface's own, his huge hand utterly enfolding Boniface's arm.

"Leon Alvisson, King of Einsamal," he echoed, voice tinny in his own ears. "Well-met."

There was a part of him that couldn't really comprehend it, that here was a magical king right in front of him, touching him as casually as if he was Boniface's very own uncle, because this wasn't for him. He wasn't meant to be here, but that was the point, wasn't it, the exchange?

"It'll get easier," the king said quietly, his voice kind, before he clapped his hands together so hard the sound was like a thunderclap, making Boniface flinch. "Fenris, lad, here's Virtue's boy!"

He shoved Boniface in the centre of his back, making him stumble into the arena. The boys had split apart from their play with one another, and it was the two smaller ones that approached him at first, both of them staring at him with focus in their eyes, slight smirks pulling at their lips.

They had light brown eyes and dark hair, both of them with natural highlights through the swept back waves — they moved in synchronicity with one another, taking slow, loping steps like wolves or wild cats, and Boniface swallowed, standing still in his place as they approached him, then crossed over right in front of him.

They walked past him on his either side, and he didn't know if he should look to the left or the right, glancing at one of them and then the other, but the big boy was approaching now, so Boniface looked forward.

He had a serious face, strong eyebrows, a strong jaw, and his eyes were a pale, shining brown that seemed almost solid in colour from this far away. He moved with slow, predatory intent, his lips pressed together, every step utterly silent on the dirt as he came forward, into Boniface's space.

Boniface had to look up at him — he wasn't a particularly small boy, was average height, but the prince — Fenris — was big.

He stood right in front of Boniface, his chin up, his expression cold, glaring down at him, and Boniface swallowed hard.

"You're the exchange?" he asked, and Boniface had almost expected him to rumble in the way that his father did, but he didn't, had a normal boy's voice even though he was so big.

"I, yes," said Boniface, and put out his hand, straightening his back as best he could. His voice cracked slightly as he said, "Well-met."

The boy stared down at him with such a hardness in his face that Boniface almost shuddered, but then his face changed: all of a sudden, he was beaming, and it was as though the sun radiated out of his face, as though he were pure brightness and shine, and Boniface felt himself relax.

"Welcome!" said Fenris, grabbing his arm, and then he pulled Boniface closer, making him let out a breathless sound as their chests knocked together. Fenris squeezed him with all the strength of a bear, lifting him off his feet and making him laugh, and Boniface tried to wrestle free and almost managed it, stumbling back before Fenris grabbed him around the neck and pulled him in again. "Oh, he's strong!"

"Let me— Ah, hey!" Boniface cried out, voice muffled against Fenris' belly, and he couldn't force his way out of Fenris' grip, but couldn't really twist himself out either: he'd wrestled and play-fought with other boys all his life, wasn't as into it as some people were but enjoyed it from time to time, but... With someone like Fenris?

It wasn't exactly easy.

He went suddenly limp, no longer keeping himself upright, and while he had no doubt that Fenris could easily pick him up, suddenly supporting all of Boniface's weight took him by surprise, and he lost his grip.

When Boniface hit the floor it was on his side, jarring his elbow, but he rolled over and scrambled back as best he could, stumbling back from Fenris. Fenris was staring at him with his mouth open, genuine surprise writ on his features, and Boniface was worried for a second that he'd offended, but then he started laughing again, and clapped — his father was clapping too.

"Well done," he said, "my boy is stronger than you are — it's right that you should attempt some cunning and take him by surprise. What do you think, Frum? Can you make something of him?"

"Frum?" Boniface repeated, and then felt his shoulders hit something. He turned to see not another boy, but a young man who had to be about twenty or so, although it was difficult to tell with how thick his beard was and with what a dramatic mane of hair he had. He had severe features, a permanent scowl pulling at his lips, and looking down at Boniface, he glanced to the king, then nodded.

"This is Frum," said Fenris. "He guards my brother and I, and trains us too — and these two are Lux and Umbra, they're close friends of mine, and we'll all be seeing a lot of each other."

"Your brother?" asked Boniface, and Fenris nodded, and gestured.

Frum and Fenris' brother must have been on the other side of the arena before, because Boniface saw him approaching from behind Frum, and felt his mouth fall open.

Fenris looked like a viking boy, as much as Boniface could estimate what a viking would look like — he wore a brown cloth shirt over skirts he was fighting in, darker leggings, a huge belt around his waist, and his friends were dressed the same, but not this boy. He wore robes, the same as Is did: a long blue robe that came down to his ankles over top of a darker blue tunic, open at the chest and belted across the middle. He looked like a wizard in a storybook, just as Fenris looked like a viking.

He was taller than his brother, but square and slim rather than big and brawny, and where Fenris had thick swathes of very dark brown hair that had threatened to burst out of his bun even before he let it free, his brother's was black. It was thinner hair, too, thinner and finer and shinier, and where Fenris' hair was swept back from his big head in a heavy mane now he'd pulled it out of his bun, his brother's hair hung around his shoulders, falling over them like a waterfall over stone.

He had different coloured eyes, which Boniface had never seen before — one was a pale brown colour, the same as Fenris', and the other was a darker, surprisingly vibrant green. He was paler than Fenris, and he had larger eyes — where Fenris' eyes were single-lidded, his brother's were double-lidded with the eyelid being very heavy, making it almost look as though he were half-closing his eyes.

It was strange, looking between the two of them — Boniface would have been able to tell right away that they were brothers, seeing the similarities between their faces, because they did look like one another, but comparing this boy's face to Prince Fenris and King Leon, he would have been hard-pressed to find a detail that was actually the same between the three of them.

The whole face resembled theirs, but all the small details of his features were different.

"My name is Loptr," he said quietly. "Welcome to Einsamal, Boniface. Don't dwell overmuch on the difficulty of your crossing — you'll find that the seas around the island are calmer than those between our two nations, and might not trouble your stomach in the same way."

Boniface had never seen a boy that looked like Loptr did — he seemed to be the same age as they were, but somehow he seemed infinite and ancient and really quite impressive, exuded a field of energy that Boniface didn't feel equipped to breach until Loptr gripped his arm.

His hand was cold and strong.

"I love your eyes," Boniface blurted out. "I've never seen that before."

"Heterochromia," said Loptr, drawing back his hand even though Boniface almost hoped he'd hug him the same way Fenris had hugged him.

"Loptr is a child of Loki," said Umbra good-naturedly.

"What, literally?" asked Boniface, feeling his eyebrows raise and a slight smile on his face — Lux and Umbra laughed, and Fenris smiled, but he'd said the wrong thing, because Loptr's expression went cold, and he put his lips together.

"This business attended to, Father, if I might be excused?" he asked, looking at King Leon over Boniface's shoulder, and Leon waved him off without seeming to approve, but he made no complaint as Loptr turned and walked away, the robe he was wearing shifting like Is' did when she walked.

"I offended him?" asked Boniface as he turned to look at the other boys, and Fenris shook his head.

"My brother keeps his own company, that's all," said Fenris, wrapping his big arm around Boniface's shoulder. "He is under stress, and he has a naturally cool demeanour — please, don't think ill of him. He will warm to you."

He was tugged around the neck back into the ring, the three boys standing in front of him.

"Come, then," said Leon, leaning on the arena fence. "Show us what you can do."

"Nothing," said Boniface.

Leon laughed. "We'll see!"

Boniface dodged as Fenris lunged at him, and was surprised by the laugh that eked out of his throat as he put up his hands to keep the other boy from grabbing at his head.

* * *

Loptr's boots made little sound on the stone flooring, his feet as quiet as a cat's, but Mother still stirred in her bed as he came through the doorway, bowing his head and ducking under the curtain that separated it from the main corridor. The room was dark, only a little light coming in from the mostly-clothed skylight to the room's edge, and the little light served to make her look almost luminescently pale.

He couldn't decide which was worse — in the dark, she seemed white as bone, but in the light, you could see the yellow-green tint of jaundice to her skin, the gauntness of her face put into less obvious relief with no dramatic shadows at her cheeks or beneath her eyes, but the bones themselves almost visible through her papery skin. Neither was right, and neither matched up to what he remembered from his childhood, when she was a rosy-cheeked woman, plump and always smiling.

"What's he like?" she asked, her voice hoarse and quiet — he had to strain to hear her, but that was not unusual these days.

"He's human," said Loptr, washing his hands at the basin and drying them off. "He lacks a real aura of his own — I expect that will change with time."

"It always does."

"He's trying very hard not to show his fear," said Loptr, thinking of the boy that had come forward, his head always tipping forward slightly, his eyes naturally casting down, and the focus with which he had kept lifting them again to meet his father's gaze, Fenris' gaze, the gazes of Frum and Lux and Umbra and, yes, Loptr himself. "He's nervous — this is all quite unlike the life he has come from, but he seems motivated to display some pride. He cares for his family's reputation, perhaps, or that of Virtue's — or even his own, but I don't know. He seems younger than we are."

"Younger than Lux and Umbra?" asked his mother, voice almost creaking on her breaths, and Loptr closed his eyes, trying not to flinch at the sound of it. "Younger than Fenris? Or just younger than you, dear?"

"He'll be smaller than they are," said Loptr, ignoring the jab and pouring tea. "Built more like me, perhaps, though not as tall — he'll be handsome."

"You saw a vision?"

"An echo of the future over the face he has, that's all," Loptr demurred, and brought a tray with two cups over to the bed, setting them down. He watched his mother's hand twitch slightly, saw her flex her tired fingers, but although she'd managed to lift herself up to recline upright against the pillows, she didn't seem fit today to lift the cup herself, and Loptr picked it up for her, bringing it up to her mouth, letting her blow on it before she took a sip. "As of now, there's a roundness to his features that will be carved away with the years and time in the arena — his jaw will harden and cut a strong line, his cheeks will strengthen. His eyes will deepen in their colour, become an emerald where they're now a mossy green, as his brow strengthens, as more light is allowed in them. His hair is going to darken, too — it's a brighter blond now, but time will render it more like the gold of brown wheat under sun, a darker, richer colour."

"He sounds like he'll be handsome," said Mother. "A shame I won't get to see him."

Loptr opened his mouth, then thought better of it, and set her cup down.

"You'll see a little of it, here and there," he said, and she looked at him in surprise, her brows furrowing.

"I will?"

"He'll come in here," said Loptr, looking across the room and seeing the golden shimmer in the doorway — the ghost was many layered and nondescript, but having been introduced to the other boy, he could see Boniface's echo there, in amongst that of his own, of Father and Fenris', of different servants and friends and healers. "A few times."

"Will you invite him in?" asked Mother.

"No," said Loptr. "I don't expect so."

Mother moved slightly on the bed, her head against the pillows, and she looked at Loptr seriously, her hand resting on her belly. "You don't see the — You don't see events, do you? Things that will happen?"

"Not really," said Loptr. "I see visions of what will be in the way we see a reflection from the pond in fog or mist — it's filmy and coloured by light, unstable, and it hurts my eyes to really concentrate on it. Echoes of people's faces, the scars they'll get, where they'll be and where they won't. I'm not a true diviner, Mother."

"What do you see when you look at your reflection, Loptr?"

"I see myself, Mother," said Loptr. "As most people do."

"No one's ever beside you?" she asked. There was a quiet hope in her voice, but it was hindered by an exhausted dreaminess, and he didn't answer her as her head tipped further into her pillows, her eyes closing deeper. By the time she woke up, hours later, she'd forgotten the question — she barely remembered their conversation at all.

* * *

The ball was a triumph for the ages, which was only fitting — it had been some three or four years since the palace had last hosted a soirée as significant as this one, with so many visiting dignitaries in attendance, and Boniface was overwhelmed by it, the wide variety of dresses and suits in the room, all those shimmering fabrics, beautiful heads of silken hair, made-up faces...

He'd been twelve when he'd first stepped foot on Einsamal Isle. He'd been picked by lottery from the other boys in his year at school — it was an old custom, not practised in most of Alba or Cymru-Loegr these days, but Virtue was a separate magical state, and the only way they really maintained that state separation from the twinned kingdoms was because they were given significant protection by Einsamal and allied fae kingdoms, and the only way to maintain *that* was...

It had been a century since the last pick, and she'd never come back, was now living on the other side of the island and taming dragons — but Stellan, the Einsamal boy who'd come to Virtue in exchange a hundred years ago, had never gone back home either. He was head librarian at the university even now, a tall man with tattoos that rippled from his wrists up to his neck, had a thick beard, and sapphires glinting in his eyes.

In theory, Boniface had been here for twelve years. He looked about twenty-four or twenty-five, anyway, and felt about that age as much as he could grasp that sort of feeling, and that was how much time had passed for his parents, his family in Virtue.

It had been—

How was he supposed to know?

Fae peoples didn't much keep track of time, least of all somewhere like Einsamal Isle, where the air was so thick with magic that even the slow time of fae lands flowed slower than treacle, and he'd given up counting the days. If you did that, you'd only end up going mad.

The girl they'd sent in exchange had been the only daughter of a noble family, because Boniface's mother was a cardiothoracic surgeon and his father was head of Virtue's Treasury. The children exchanged were meant to be of approximately equal value — what that had meant when he'd arrived was a soft feather bed and a room decorated in tapestries, a house hung with portraits and hundreds upon hundreds of heirlooms and antiques, and—

Horse-riding lessons.

Horse-riding lessons, and sword-fighting lessons, his own rapier, fitted armour, and all the rest.

It wasn't as though he were the only human on the island. The royals were human once, a few hundred years ago, before they'd come into fae lands on a fucking longship, and they still looked human now, for the most part. Unless you knew they weren't, you'd probably never realise, seeing them walk down a mundie street somewhere like Virtue, but of course, that was unlikely to happen.

The party was in full swing.

Boniface was standing on one of the balconies and the crown prince was laughing his bellowing laugh, gripping one of his fellows on the upper arm and shaking his hand before they looked once again to the dice game between them on the table.

Down on the main floor, Boniface could see the second prince speaking seriously with a contingent from the Queen's lands, standing straight, gesturing with his hands in neat, crisply choreographed moments, never drawing his arms too far from his chest. He always moved like that.

He must have felt Boniface's gaze on him, because he turned his head slightly and met his eyes, and Boniface looked away.

"Bonny," said Fenris, and caught Boniface's cheek under his huge, muscled palm, radiating a heat so wonderfully full that it didn't burn or scorch where it touched Boniface's cheek, but felt like the warmest sunlight. "You're in one of your pensive moods."

"Am I, highness?" asked Boniface, grinning, and he shoved his way into the midst of the warrior men, shoving between Lux and Umbra and sweeping up the dice from the table. "My apologies!"

Fenris laughed, clapped his mighty hands together, and they played.

He'd learned to play a lot of gambling games over the last few decades — dice games and card games, boardgames, and he distantly remembered being a little boy and playing videogames, having a games console, but he couldn't remember what it was called, couldn't really remember what exactly the appeal had been compared to other games.

All of that was a long time ago, a literal world away, and he wasn't a child of Virtue anymore, wasn't the man he would have been if he'd never left to come here.

He was now a member of his highness' *retinue*, and Boniface thought sometimes how strange it was, that as a child he had envisioned a life for himself wholly unlike the one he got, a fantasy dream, something out of a children's book, and yet for him, all the *adventure* was... Routine.

To be expected.

Last week he'd put a dagger through the heart of a mist wolf, killed it dead after it had caught the scent of a man in the village and begun to lurk the streets at night, hunting men when it should have been hunting the beasts of the woods — and he'd hauled it over his shoulder, carried its corpse into the village and people had *cheered*.

How could he have envisioned that, as a little boy? How could he have known he'd ever do something like that?

"Hello, your highness," he said once he was down on the floor, and Loptr turned to look at him. His hair was braided up in complicated lines, interwoven with thin chains and shining pins, but Boniface almost preferred it the way he ordinarily wore it, loose around his shoulders with beads woven in. This was too ornate, really, made Loptr look like he belonged on a shelf rather than in the field with the rest of them.

They were about the same age, or so it had seemed to Boniface when they'd met, but no matter how hard he tried, Loptr never wanted anything to do with him as a child, as a teenager, and that had changed very little now. Over the years, Loptr had warmed to Boniface about as much as Boniface had accustomed to travelling by sea — that was to say, not at all.

"Boniface," said Loptr in his smooth, cool tones.

His brother's eyes were almond-shaped and single-lidded, and he was more handsome than Loptr was — his skin was darker, had a warmer colour to it, and his lips were thinner but more defined. Loptr was much paler than his brother, so pale that his skin seemed almost transparent in places, pink lining showing around his mouth and his eyes and where his skin was at its thinnest; he had long eyelashes and heavy double eyelids, so much so that his eyes seemed permanently half-closed, but Boniface had learned very early on that for all appearances, Loptr was always wide-awake, most of all when it seemed like he was sleeping.

They looked the same. He didn't know how, still didn't understand it, but Loptr looked like his brother and his father when they were stood side by side, their features occupying the same space despite being so different.

"You're not dancing," said Boniface softly. "I don't suppose I can tempt you?"

"What could you possibly tempt me with?" asked Loptr, his expression revealing nothing.

"About the same as what I tempt anybody with," said Boniface. "My charm and good company."

"One would think you would learn to raise the stakes," said Loptr, and Boniface was surprised that he should say it, feeling his lips shift into a smile, his eyebrows raising. He stepped closer, and while a part of him regretted it — Loptr's eyes flitted down to his feet and his expression stiffened slightly, although he didn't lean back — he was thrilled by the idea that Loptr should meet his flirtation head-on for once.

He was mad, he knew that. He was mad and stupid besides.

He didn't know what it was about Loptr that so enchanted him, so engaged him, after all these decades chasing after him — Loptr was a solitary man by nature, and while occasionally he joined the retinue when they went on one journey or other, or could be pressured into coming to an alehouse if Fenris pushed him, most of the time if Boniface so much as wanted to look at him, he had to seek him out.

It used to be he'd spend long hours looking after his mother, who had been ill for years on end, and a few times over the past few years Boniface had met her, always settled beneath her blankets with her face drawn and her body weak.

She'd been a kind woman, Queen Ingrid. He'd always wished going to see her that he might learn more about her, what she had been and who she was before she became ill, but she was always tremendously weak and could rarely speak at length; Boniface had always done his best to charm her, to tell her stories of her stepson or what little he could of Loptr, to make her smile.

It was one of the only times that Boniface was able to make Loptr smile himself: by nature, he was a serious man, quiet and reserved, and it seemed to Boniface that apart from Fenris, only his mother had been able to make him smile. Even Leon never seemed to manage it, but then, Boniface didn't see him try — the king always seemed to meet Loptr on his own terms, spoke to him very seriously, didn't play with him as he did with Fenris.

Loptr read complex tomes that seemed older than the island; he spent long hours skinning animals and harvesting alchemy ingredients from their carcasses, doing various complex apothecarian experiments; he went for long walks alone, and only a few times over the years Boniface had managed to go with him on these.

He'd chatter as they moved, speaking at length even as Loptr said almost nothing, and sometimes they'd settle into silence together that Boniface could almost imagine was companionable, except for the fact that Boniface could bring Loptr flowers every day (he'd tried this for a month as a sixteen-year-old) or serenade him with love songs (he'd tried multiple times over the years) or just tell him, frankly and honestly, that he was beautiful in a way no other men were (he'd gotten out "I wanted to tell you—" before Loptr walked away from him), and Loptr would only ever treat him with scorn and distaste.

"What should I raise the stakes with?" asked Boniface quietly. "What of mine might I bet you, your highness, that you might like to win?"

"Good point," said Loptr scathingly, his anger surprising. "You have nothing."

Loptr's stare was cold, a heavy weight on Boniface's face, and as soon as Boniface broke eye contact with him, unable not to deflate when faced with a comment like that, Loptr was walking away.

Boniface sighed, and when a handsome young woman from the Camelot contingent looked his way, he caught her eye, beamed, gave a bow. When she extended her hand to him, he took it, and brushed the back of her knuckles with his lips.

The night went on — he didn't lay eyes on Loptr again.

* * *

For the fourth night in just as many, Loptr woke in the middle of the night, gasping and shuddering. His body was soaked with sweat, his hair tangled about his head in knots of uncomfortable, twisting strands — he'd been thrashing awfully, evidently, and as he stumbled from his bed and cast out with magic to set his bath to run, he combed it out with his fingers, as gentle as he could manage.

There was nausea unsettling his gut, but he hadn't woken up retching, and he managed to keep his stomach settled as he went to the doorway to the bath, putting his forehead against the doorframe.

He heard the cloth hangings rustle, and he kept his body angled away as he turned his head until he realised it was Fenris, and relaxed. It was one thing for the palace staff to know he had nightmares — they didn't need to see him soaked with sweat and naked into the mix, looking as haggard as he did.

"You shouted," Fenris mumbled through a yawn, half-collapsed against the other frame himself. "Are you well, brother?"

"Uneasy dreams, that's all," lied Loptr. "I'm going to bathe, and that will soothe me. Good night."

"Good night," Fenris echoed, and Loptr saw him hesitate a moment, opening his mouth, but then he seemed to think better of it and left Loptr be, which Loptr was grateful for. Fenris almost always left him to his own business, if he asked to be.

The bath was filled from the mountain spring, and it filled very quickly, steam filling the air until Loptr shut the sluice gate and climbed into the bath. The hot water immediately soothed his skin, eking into his muscles and making him relax, and he sighed as he sank into the water to his neck, continuing to reach up and comb through his hair with his fingers.

It used to be he slept so very easily, and it was strange, but he really couldn't remember how it had felt. Oh, yes, he slept. He knew he had slept — he would climb into bed and set his head on the pillow and sleep would come, and certainly he must have had pleasant dreams, because he remembered talking about them. He didn't particularly remember being well-rested or sleeping well, but the fact that he didn't remember it was precisely because it had been so very ordinary.

The nightmares that plagued him now were Fenris', by rights — it used to be he was so frightened to sleep at night he couldn't bear to be in bed alone, and Loptr remembered when first he had begun to have them, how he would wake in the night to see Fenris asleep beside him, shaking and moving erratically. Rarely would he climb into Loptr's bed, because Loptr sprawled in his sleep and Fenris never wanted to disturb him, but he would sleep on the bench at the foot of it, or on the chaise to one edge of the room.

It had been natural to take the nightmares on, entirely natural. Fenris was the elder brother as far went years and blood, but what mattered years and blood to a mage? It fell to Loptr to protect his brother, the crown prince, shield him from all that would ail him, and shield him he did, even from this.

They were worsening, as the years passed.

It was the curse of his mother's bloodline that had sent Fenris' own mother mad, that she walk out into the mists of Einsamal and disappear into the mountains. Loptr had never met her, but Father had described her to him, from time to time, how she had been when first he met her, how strong and commanding she'd been, Sigrid with her thick arms and lionish smile and her axe always at the ready.

She'd wielded that axe against Leon, against Fenris even, before she'd run off into the night.

Loptr had read the old accounts — it was the father of Sigrid's grandfather who had trespassed through a sacred woodland some realms away, and a further trespass than that, killed a sacred elk. Everyone that had eaten of its meat had become infected with a strange and terrible madness, one that began in dreams but slowly escalated, bleeding into their waking lives, and each of those passed it onto their firstborn children.

Of course, none of them had been mages, none of them trained in the arts of false dreams or inured to the infectious madnesses that accompanied some magics and rituals, as Loptr was, as he had been trained to be.

And if the curse did overtake him, if he was driven mad by it—

It would be his death that came of it, and not Fenris', as was right. This was his duty.

It was beginning to be unwieldy, though, keeping him up at all hours no matter when he tried to sleep, and time and time again he would wake up vomiting or otherwise haggard. It wasn't as though he wanted to die, or wanted to be driven mad — it was simply that he saw no reason to allow Fenris to be, when Fenris was to be king.

He ducked his head under the water, and for a few moments just lingered there with the weight of the heat on his head, around his hair, feel the pressure in his lungs as he held his breath.

It was untenable, he knew.

Mother had told him that she hadn't been helping with the weight of it — he'd demanded of her more than once if she was, if she was taxing herself to help him, and every time he'd asked, she'd denied it. He was certain now that this was a lie: when Mother had died, the nightmares had amplified immeasurably overnight.

It probably killed her sooner, taking the tax of that curse on her. And for what? For—

He raised his head from the water and heaved in a breath, filling his lungs.

Untenable, yes. Tomorrow—

Tomorrow. Tomorrow, he'd see what he could do to make it easier.

* * *

Boniface was in the yard when his highness came calling — it was a fine, sunny day, a warmth in the air and salt hanging on the breeze as it came in from over the sea, and he was tending to Buttermilk, bringing the brush over her sides and feeling her relax underneath his hands before he dropped it aside and lifted the saddle onto her back.

Fenris could ride bareback, of course, and always did — he had a strange way with animals, a way of communicating with even the wildest of them, so that Boniface had seen him ride not just horses but elk and giant snakes and fae wolves, big mighty creatures that seemed almost too big to ride.

The others in his retinue — Lux and Umbra and Frum — rode horseback and normally used saddles, but as far as Boniface knew, they could ride without a saddle just like Fenris could.

He had been *taught,* theoretically, or at least he'd had lessons — his foster parents had insisted he give it a try, but it never felt solid and easy like they said it was supposed to, never felt like it wasn't dangerous, wasn't precarious. He preferred the saddle. He felt stable in the saddle, especially when they were riding as fast as they did, or when they were fighting.

King Leon said that riding bareback gave them more flexibility in the field, but the only flexibility Boniface saw in it was in being thrown to the ground to the left or the right, and he didn't much see the appeal.

"Where are you riding?" asked a voice beside him, and Boniface turned to look at Loptr as he approached.

Loptr normally wore a mage's robes — tunics were common fare around here, and most men wore some sort of tunic over leggings, although Boniface preferred to wear a real shirt and breeches. Mages and elders tended to wear a longer robe, the skirt stopping around the mid-calf or ankles instead of the mid-thigh. Even when they were children, Loptr had dressed like that, dressed like a man a few hundred years his senior — worn layers of robes with a belt around his waist, a chatelaine or knives on his belt.

He was dressed now to ride, white chemise tucked into black leather breeches, wearing an open vest overtop of the shirt. Boniface almost never saw black leather here in these islands — people tended not to dye it at all, or wore fae leathers that were more interesting colours, but when Loptr wore black leather, it was blacker than black.

He dyed it himself in some sort of drake venom, and Boniface knew from having seen people fight him in the arena that it carried a pretty strong magical charge, one that Loptr could prime to set off like a detonated blast.

"I was just going to ride in the hills," said Boniface.

"You aren't accompanying my brother abroad?"

"They're sailing," said Boniface. "You know I get seasick, highness."

"One of your many weaknesses," said Loptr coolly, and Boniface pressed his lips together, doing his best not to clench his teeth. "If you will stoop from your ordinary dedication to the crown prince, I would commission your services."

Boniface stared at him. "Stoop to... You want me to go with you somewhere?"

"I require a second rider," said Loptr. "I'll ask nothing challenging of you — I need only someone to watch guard and send word back to the palace in the case I take too long to return."

Boniface grinned, stepping closer — Loptr was taller than he was (everyone was taller than he was) but it still pleased him to lean up and into Loptr's space, tipping back and forth on his feet, unable not to grin. "You want *me*?" he asked, almost crowed. "Me, highness?"

"Any other peasant boy will do," said Loptr. "If you won't deign to offer your services, I can—"

"No, no, of course I will," said Boniface immediately. "My life belongs to the crown, highness — your hand or your brother's, it's all the same to me."

"How unflattering," said Loptr, and Boniface frowned at him, but Loptr was already walking away, clicking his tongue and summoning forth the stallion he always rode, a big black beast with hair as sleek and shiny as the leather Loptr wore.

His saddle was black too.

"Come, then," said Loptr, pulling himself up astride and tossing his hair over one shoulder. "Let us ride."

Boniface shook his head, but as frustrating as Loptr's terse personality was, he couldn't deny he was flattered to be called on, for Loptr to come to him. Pulling himself up and astride Buttermilk, he pushed for her to follow after the prince, and for a while they rode through the roads that led away from the city proper, out onto the paths that led into the mountain forests.

Einsamal was a large island, but there was no point trying to measure it with miles or kilometres — portals and borders were dotted all through its forests and up through its mountain pathways, and it was easy indeed to go through a gateway and end up somewhere you had never been before, although not always so easy to find your way back. It was a land thick with magic and made of many-layered places, and while Boniface considered himself familiar with most of the island's main paths, knew a great many shortcuts and beautiful, hidden places that a lay of the evening would be suitably entranced by, he kept close to Loptr, making sure he was leading the way as they rode.

"Is all well with you?" he asked when they came to a point on the path where it was possible to ride side-by-side, and Loptr didn't even look at him, his gaze forward.

"If it wasn't, what would you do about it?"

"Whatever was in my power to do, highness."

"Nothing, then," said Loptr, and Boniface sighed, looking away from Loptr's blank expression for a moment and instead looking out over the crystal-blue waters of the sea far beneath them.

When Boniface had only been about fourteen, he and the rest of the retinue had accompanied Fenris to a cliff edge not far from here and Boniface had barely been able to watch as the other boys had dived far below into the waters, and then climbed up the cliff face with their bare palms and feet. He knew that Loptr wouldn't make him do that — on the day they'd gone there, it was Loptr who'd stayed up on the grass with Boniface. He'd barely looked at him, had just sat back on his bedroll and paged through a book, but it had comforted Boniface that he'd been there, that he hadn't been alone.

"Is there a reason you hate me so?" Boniface asked in idle tones when they turned away from the coastal paths and headed further inland, beginning to ascend into the mountains. "Something I've done to offend you at some point?"

When Loptr didn't answer, he craned forward in his saddle to better look at his face, and Loptr caught him looking and clucked his tongue, rolling his eyes. "You're a self-centred fool, Boniface. Just because I don't fall over myself to worship you or coo over your songs and your sword skills, you think I hate you?"

"You seem to hate everybody," said Boniface, and Loptr set his jaw, but didn't reply, and they rode on. "This is within a day's ride?"

"An hour or so, no more."

"Why do you need a paltry *peasant boy* as your accompaniment, then?"

"Because I wanted to be pelted with pointless questions, evidently."

"Oh, forgive me," said Boniface sarcastically. "So honoured am I to be in the rare presence of his highness, the prince, that I speak without thought."

"When *do* you speak with thought?"

"You're right, of course, what brains have I compared to yours? Each and every one of us on this isle is stupid compared to *you*, o prince, so impressive and unbeatable is your insight. You, an immortal, a genius, where the rest of us are simply ants beneath your feet."

He'd evidently struck a nerve, because Loptr's head whipped to the side with a snarl pulling at his thin lips, but he seemed to think better of it, get better control of himself, because before he could say anything he looked forward again, and urged his horse to ride a little faster. Boniface kept pace.

It used to be he was frightened to talk back to Loptr.

He didn't know when the levee had broken, when he'd changed his mind, gained a bit of confidence — it wasn't while he was a child, not even when he was an older teenager, he didn't think, couldn't have been until he was at least eighteen or nineteen and realised that if he actually snapped at Loptr, the other man wouldn't do a thing to harm him, and was liable even to respond more than he would if Boniface tried to stay polite.

Oh, it would never do in public — Loptr was the *prince*, after all, and Boniface only a member of his brother's retinue, and he'd never get away with it there, let alone in front of Fenris, but when the two of them were alone? There was no reason he shouldn't be, from time to time, as cutting with Loptr as Loptr was with him.

"Always cold, aren't you?" Boniface asked, and he heard the bitterness in his voice, but it was too late to hold it back. "The world would simply end if you accepted someone's hand of friendship."

"I don't need your friendship."

"Oh, you don't need anything," said Boniface dryly. "That's why we're riding off somewhere in secret on a day your brother just happens to be off the island. Nothing untoward about this, is there?"

Loptr's expression was a study in blankness, revealing nothing.

"If you wish to turn back," he said quietly — too quietly, too cool, too controlled — "you may do so."

"I'm in your service, highness," Boniface retorted. "I would no more turn back now than I'd lay a hand on you."

"Ha," said Loptr, almost a bark of laughter, but there was no mirth in it.

"What?" Boniface asked, and Loptr turned his head now, arching one perfect eyebrow, his perfect eyes cold, his perfect lips curled in a snarl that was entirely superior.

"You think every night of laying your hands on me," said Loptr, voice so icy that Boniface actually shivered, and he ducked his head, breaking the prince's gaze. "And you wonder why I have no want of your friendship."

"Apologies, highness," muttered Boniface. "So *argr* as you are, I'd no idea you'd take offence being desired as such."

"Don't echo words you don't know the implications of," said Loptr, almost seeming pleased as he sat back in the saddle and raised his head. Boniface's belly was a mess of snakes, and his tongue felt stuck fast in his mouth. "You don't know the meaning of *ergi*."

"Don't I? You don't think I hear what the boys say about me? What they say about *you*?"

"What do they say about you?" asked Loptr, and his mood seemed to have changed, like he was holding back laughter, but it wasn't as simple as that. There was almost a mania in it, his hands gripping tight at his horse's reins and his eyes flitting quickly back and forth over the paths ahead of them. They were under the cover of a thick woodland now, and as they rode on, Boniface was aware of how they were growing taller and taller, how there was a thickness to the air, filmy and slick and electric, sticking to his teeth. "That you can't grow a full beard?"

One of Boniface's hands went from the reins to his face, feeling the thickness of his moustache and his goatee, and Loptr laughed, shaking his head.

"You can't grow a beard at all," muttered Boniface. "Or is it different for you?"

"I can grow a beard," said Loptr, glancing at him sideways. "I shave every morning. What gave you the idea I didn't?"

Boniface opened his mouth, but as soon as he realised the word "perfect" was in the sentence that threatened to fall out of it, he closed it again. Loptr gave him a funny look, brow furrowing, but then he nodded with his head and gestured for Boniface to follow him off the main path and down a narrower one.

They had to go in single-file, and Boniface stared at Loptr's shoulders and the back of his hair as they rode, slower now, and he stroked his palm over Buttermilk's neck, letting out a low, soothing sound.

"Why don't you?" demanded Boniface, and Loptr didn't turn around.

"Why don't I what?"

"I've *heard* people say you look like a woman," said Boniface. "That you preen over yourself like a woman, that your face is shaved like a woman, that if you fuck at all, it's to let men fuck between your thighs."

Loptr laughed, and it sounded close to the warm, easy laughter he used to let out when it was just the two of them and his mother, close enough that Boniface was surprised, surprised and felt hollow and strange and painfully eager. That was how he always felt with Loptr, by and by — what was it about the man that had such a fucking hold over him?

"What are you laughing about now?"

"Nothing, nothing," said Loptr. "Just that you think of yourself as this modern man from such an impressive, *contemporary* society, all of your phones and computers and what-not. And here you are, spouting insults from an era millennia gone."

"I've *heard* people—"

"I'm sure you have," Loptr interrupted him. "Is that why you fuck every man and woman you lay eyes on, hm, to show off your virility?"

"Is there a reason you keep track of the men and women I spend my time with?" retorted Boniface. "Jealousy, maybe?"

"Here," said Loptr, all humour abruptly gone from his voice, and Boniface's breath hitched as they came into a place where the forest opened upward and outward, showing a clearing with an old temple in it.

It wasn't the sort of place he'd grown used to over the years, wasn't an open altar or a statue — columns hewn of rough grey stone led up to the temple proper, which was made of similar big slabs grown over with moss, and the ivy that ran all over it was hanging down in strands over the arch of the doorway.

It looked dark inside.

"Your highness," said Boniface quietly, not dismounting as he watched Loptr get down from his horse, tethering her to an old log and summoning a trough from what seemed like the ether, but must have been nearby because it had the same moss on it the stone pillars did. It filled with water under Loptr's shifting palm, and Boniface pulled himself down. "Your highness," he said again, louder this time.

The magic was so thick here he almost couldn't stand it, and it did more than just stick to his teeth — it filled his mouth, slid over his tongue like his mouth was full of slugs, made his nose feel full, his ears.

His skin felt wet even though he knew it was dry, and it was heavy where it tangled in his hair, threatening to plump it up like the thick air before a storm.

"Wait here," Loptr instructed him. "If I don't come out again within an hour, ride back. Untether Fallow, and she'll follow you. Go directly to the mages' library and advise Is of my location, then accompany her to my father."

"Your highness," said Boniface a third time, feeling a pit in his stomach, and Loptr stood over him, his lips pressed loosely together, his gaze focused on Boniface's face. "I can go in with you. Please, whatever this is—"

"Wait here, Boniface," said Loptr again, his expression serious, focused. "Were it not for the fact that I thought I could trust you, I would indeed have asked some random peasant boy to assist me. You have a habit of showing yourself as reliable — don't tell me I've misjudged you."

Why should it make him feel so warm inside to have Loptr speak to him like that? His voice was quiet, intent, and there was a sweetness in it that Boniface well-knew was reserved for his horse or sometimes for his brother, not for Boniface or the likes of him. "Deftly manoeuvred, my prince," muttered Boniface, not bothering to keep the scorn out of his voice. "You know well how to pull my strings."

"You'll wait?"

"For an hour," said Boniface, although he hated to capitulate — the dread he felt in this place, this place of old, old magic was unspeakable, and he had no way of knowing what it must have felt like to Loptr, who was sensitive to magical flows, sometimes clutched at his head or wrinkled his nose or otherwise showed his discomfort when they moved through spaces that were rich with the stuff. Sometimes, on stormy nights where magic accompanied the lightning on the air, he sneezed over and over again in a row, and it made all of them laugh except Loptr, who just groaned his complaints until the storm finally gave off. "Are you in danger, highness?"

"No."

"Are you lying?"

"One hour," said Loptr, and swept down the path, bowed his head, and ducked under the curtain of ivy into the stone building. Looking up to the sky, noting where the sun was, Boniface took in a breath, then set down on the log, stroking Buttermilk's cheeks when she put her head in his lap, and touched their foreheads together.

* * *

As soon as Loptr crossed the threshold into the old building he stumbled forward, dropping his shoulder against one of the great walls and heaving in a deep breath, his arms crossed over his chest for a moment. He closed his eyes, feeling the magic flow through him — he'd felt relieved when the path had narrowed and he no longer had Boniface constantly straining to see his face, too far ahead of him on the path.

He felt too hot, and the air was so thick and heated as to feel like moving through syrup — that was the right word, because there was a sweetness in it too, an enticing thrum that encouraged him to reach out and lose himself in it, drown himself in it, taste its depths and draw them into his own body until he was gorged on it.

The inside of the building was cavernous in a way one could never make out from outside, and stone steps led down into what was, some thousand years ago, an arena, the stone benches curving around and around with steps leading down between the circles of them.

The circular centre had been dirt, when first he'd come here as a child in his mother's arms, but he'd laid down grass seeds and flowers, and he'd tended this place quite regularly — practising here alone, or when Mother brought him here for his lessons.

There was a stone plinth in the centre of it, what he sometimes used as a potting table or a desk, although once or twice before, he'd fallen asleep on it, dozed on it at midday when sun came down directly through the skylight hewn in the structure's roof, ushering the light in.

Loki was sitting back on it, his legs hanging down, his palms resting slightly behind him on the stone.

He hadn't been here in a little over a year, and the thickness of the magic was almost too much for him to bear, crackling in his veins, threatening to fizzle out of his mouth, his ears, his eyes, and Loptr stumbled slightly as he descended the stairs, wishing there was a bar or a banister he could lean on, but of course, there wasn't.

"The last time I was here," said Loki in a soft and easy voice as Loptr's feet touched on the grass, feeling it thick and soft under his boots, forget-me-nots scattered here and there, smatterings of blue in amongst the green, "it was sand beneath my feet — sand stained red with blood. These benches were full of jeering crowds. Look at what you've done to the place. It was naught but dead stone and clean dirt for centuries, and you're turning it green with grass and moss."

"You have some objection to the colour green, my lord?" asked Loptr, doing his best to stand straight and look at him properly, with all the respect he was due, even though Loki showed no return of the sentiment. He stayed sprawled back, his feet bouncing, kicking loosely against the air. He was tall and strong, with thick muscle to his arms, and he had thick swathes of red hair, in which were braided charms and pendants. He wore open robes made of torn layers of dark fabric, a belt banding his waist, and there were dozens of overlapping bracelets on his wrists and a great many pendants on different lengths of chain around his neck, resting in against the orange hair dusting his chest, hints of tattoos visible under the robes he wore, and many more showing on his bare arms.

He was wearing mundie shoes — bright red trainers laced in white, with white rims around the soles.

It was not the first time Loptr had been face to face with him — he'd given to him directly in one temple or another, at festivals before. He'd given to other figures, other divinities, but so had Fenris, so had Father, so had Mother — it was only Loptr that gave to Loki.

Of the family, it was only Loptr Loki would take from.

"How could I object to the colour green, boy?" asked Loki, arching two bushy red eyebrows. "That's the colour you are, just about now."

Loptr looked down at the floor, battling against the wave of nausea that hit him — it was a lack of sleep, a lack of control, a sense of being unwell, unfinished, exhausted. He could segment himself to some extent, push down the feeling, but here in a place of such thick magic, such constant and complete magic, he couldn't segment himself whatsoever. He felt the sickly unpleasantness in its entirety, as heavily as he felt it when he woke from his nightmares, the sensation fresh and painfully heavy, sinking right into him.

"What a curious thing it is, a curious thing you are," said Loki quietly, his lips shifted into a small smile. There were scars around his lips, regular marks over the line of the top and then the bottom one, and if you really looked you'd be able to trace exactly where they'd sewn them shut; clouding his eyes in a film that Loptr could see but also couldn't see at once were more scars, whitening the skin, bleaching his eyelashes, lightening the colour of his irises and his pupils so that each eye seemed to be white at times.

Looking at one layer of film was a mistake, because suddenly he couldn't stop himself looking at all of them at once — Loki's hair and eyes rippling with sparks and fire; Loki's hair black with charcoal and his face daubed in dark grey; Loki spattered with blood, his hair a darker, deeper red; Loki made of stone, Loki made of steel, Loki made of pure agonisingly bright magic —

He blinked, and heaved in a gasp of air that hurt his lungs, because Loki was no longer in front of him but standing beside him, and he was squeezing Loptr's shoulder very hard, forcing the world to narrow down to that point, narrow down to Loki's existence, Loki's certainty, Loki beside him, but not the sight of him, not the vision he cut.

"Yes, that's what I was about to say," said Loki, and his voice was quiet but it sparked with distant thunder, thrumming through him, filling him to the brim. "Young man, upon your birth, you were allotted a madness all of your very own, no scales in those pretty-coloured eyes of yours, that you might see the world without the filters of reality through which other people see it. Is that not enough for you? You are so greedy for insanity you needed to steal someone else's madness into the bargain?"

Loptr breathed in, filling his lungs very slowly, bit by bit, to try to swallow down the wave of nausea that hit him. There was a darkness filtering in at the edges of his vision, not yet fully encroaching on him but threatening to do so sometime soon, and in the distance, some ways beyond the edges of that darkness, he heard echoing hisses and screams, a promise of a torture to come.

"My brother is heir to the throne," whispered Loptr. "It is my duty to shield him."

"Yes, you swore to your father, didn't you?" asked Loki, and Loptr jumped at the sound that suddenly echoed in the arena, so loud it hurt his ears, made his eyes feel swollen and painful, made his skin feel drawn tight as rubber between two poles.

"I swear, Father, I will take on this burden as best I can. I wouldn't have him suffer as Queen Sigrid suffered."

"You can do it?" rumbled Father's voice in response, echoing painfully through his ribcage. *"You can stopper this poison before it seeps into him?"*

"Yes. I can — I will."

"What a child of Loki you will be, my boy," purred Loki in his ear, "taking on a kenning of mine like *Oath-breaker.*"

"No," whispered Loptr, and turned to look at Loki, forced to stare at his face, his *real* face, at the freckles and scars on his skin, at the shape of his many-times broken nose, at the redness of his hair, the grey of one eye and the green of the other. "No, that's why I came here, why I begged you meet me, I'll do — I'll do whatever you ask me. Give you whatever you would demand."

Loki's face flared brightly on purpose this time, all sparks so that Loptr's eyes stung and he had to look away, but he didn't pull away from Loki's hand, didn't think he could survive without the anchor it provided in this moment.

"What are you asking me for?" asked Loki, and his voice was less mellifluous now, no longer sing-song, no longer as playful. "State your desires plainly and with frankness."

"I want this punishment stamped out of my brother's bloodline," said Loptr. "Not by his death or by his infertility, but entirely, his slate wiped clean — and I... I don't wish to suffer this madness either. I want it gone from him without taking on the burden for myself. Let me have my own madness, and let him go without — let him be prince, that he might be king."

"And if it isn't punishment?" asked Loki. "If it's no magical curse, as you've been told, but is merely the onset of some genetic predisposition, hm? A mental illness, as I'm sure you've heard of, some schizophrenic disorder?"

Loptr felt his lips downturn, his head tilting. "Is it?" he asked, and Loki laughed.

"No, no," he said, amused. "It's a curse of madness, magical in its origin and its ravages. Wouldn't you be in trouble if it wasn't, though?"

"I'm in trouble either way, my lord," said Loptr, and Loki laughed again.

"Oh, yes. I suppose you are, aren't you?"

"My lord—"

"Stop, stop, I don't care to hear begging," said Loki coolly, and pushed him gently forward until he was sitting back against the stone plinth, and Loki hopped up to sit beside him again, resting in the position he had before, one leg crossing over the other, palms to the stone, his shoulder touching Loptr's. "You understand that the price for what you're asking will be rather high, hm?"

"Yes."

"It was Odin himself against whom your brother's great-grandfather trespassed, did you know that?"

Loptr's stomach lurched. "No," he said. "No, I didn't."

"You'll have to offer me something quite significant to convince me to petition the Allfather himself for his mercy."

"My lord—"

"I told you not to beg. Have some pride, boy."

Loptr closed his mouth, staring forward, and he pressed his fingertips into his thighs, feeling the fabric of the leather, the pressure. His stomach was flipping over and over in his gut, and it had little to do, now, with the curse he was carrying with him on Fenris' behalf.

"What, then?" he asked in a whisper.

"You have a man outside. What's his name?"

Loptr felt his brow furrow, and he glanced at Loki, then looked forward, taken aback. "I — His name is Boniface. Our Virtue exchange — he traded places with Kari Astridson, and he's now a member of my brother's retinue. I only brought him with me in case..."

"In case," murmured Loki, chuckling. "In case I took you in exchange, yes? In case that was the price I demanded you pay?"

"Yes."

"And him?"

"Him? Boniface? He's nothing."

"*Nothing*?"

Loptr felt as though he were on uneven ground, unsure where this line of inquiry was going, what significance Boniface Nottingham could have to do with anything. He had no magic in him, no claim to the throne — even apart from Frum, from Lux and Umbra, he had no true binding to them, by blood or vow.

"Why did you bring him here, if he's nothing?" asked Loki.

"Because I knew he'd do as I asked of him. That he would follow my instructions — that he would fetch someone else, if needed. He's a friend of my brother's, and he's loyal to the crown."

"To you."

"As prince, yes."

"Very well," said Loki. "Here, then, to save you from becoming Oath-Breaker, and letting your brother perish despite the vow you gave your father, I will make you Betrayer. You say Boniface Nottingham is nothing? Give him to me."

Loptr turned to stare at him, no matter that it hurt his eyes, no matter that his stomach roiled. "What?"

"Give him," repeated Loki slowly, smoothly, "to me."

"But," Loptr started, and then swallowed hard, realising he was shaking his head although he didn't mean to, didn't intend to, didn't realise he was doing so until he was doing it. "He's no particular friend of mine, my lord. I feel no attachment to him whatsoever — as I said, he is of my brother's retinue, not my own. His loyalty to me is simply an extension of that attachment."

"Very well, then," said Loki, giving a nod of his head. "In that case, it should be no great hardship for you to betray him."

His head was spinning.

"Would you have asked this of anybody I brought with me?" asked Loptr. "Had I brought — Had I brought Frum, or another of Fenris' retinue, or some peasant boy from the village, would you have asked for them instead?"

"You *didn't* bring Frum, or another of your brother's retinue, or some peasant boy from the village," said Loki. "You brought him."

"But—"

"No buts," said Loki. "I will give you two days and two nights, Loptr, son of Leon, to make your decision. If you decide to avail of the pardon I might give your brother, return here before midnight the night after next and bring Boniface Nottingham to me, here. If you decide to go without, I will not make you another offer, and it is doubtful the Allfather would take a direct petition. This is your last and only chance."

Loptr's mouth tasted of copper and blood, and he swallowed hard. "Lord Loki—"

"It is not your right to ask what I would do to him," Loki interrupted him, voice cool and distant. "Nor demand some treatment, one way or another. To spare the sanity of your brother, give me his friend. If you so value his life, let your brother go mad — or let yourself go mad in your brother's place. Three paths to choose from is more than most people get, boy. Choose whichever pleases you."

Loptr turned once more to address him, but when he did, he found that Loki was gone, and he was alone in the centre of the arena.

"Fuck," he whispered. "*Fuck.*"

Taking to his feet, he moved clumsily up the steps and out into the sun again.

* * *

They rode back into Einsamal City in relative silence, Loptr barely saying a word. Twice, Boniface asked him, "What is it?" and a half a dozen times he asked, "Are you alright?" but each time Loptr waved him off, tersely shaking his head.

Fenris had still not returned to the palace when they returned, and he and the others would not be back for another day or so, and Boniface expected to go home and dine alone, in his own household, but Loptr stopped him.

"No," he said. "No, please, dine with my father and I tonight, Boniface. A thanks for your help today."

And what help, precisely, had he been?

Loptr had gone into the darkness of that stone room for what must have been half an hour, and when he'd come out again he'd been pale and sickly looking, a green pallor set over his pale skin.

"I oughtn't mention today's expedition to his majesty, I suppose?" he asked.

"I would prefer you did not. But if you do not dine with us, my father will be suspicious of my asking your company tonight."

"... I beg your pardon?"

"I do not wish to be alone tonight, Boniface," said Loptr seriously, his expression as impassive as ever, his voice intent. "If you would consent, I would have us drink together, as we've done before."

"We've never done that before," said Boniface.

Loptr's smile was thin, but real, or as real as any smile he'd ever seen from him. "As you've done with Fenris, then," he said. "Fenris and the rest of his retinue, of which I am sometimes, I might remind you, a part."

The fear came to Boniface all of a sudden, crushing, painful, tremendously cold, and he put out his hand and touched Loptr's, gripped it in his. Loptr's hand was cold, solid, but he seemed surprised to be grabbed like this, his eyes widening.

"Your highness, are you going to die?" asked Boniface. "Are you in some danger, some peril?"

Loptr exhaled slowly, and his smile was soft, warm, wholly unlike any emotion Boniface had ever seen on his face, not because of the warmth itself, because of the vulnerability it belied.

"You think," he said quietly, "that I have in some way been assured of my own peril. That, therefore, I want some last nights of comfort with a friend."

"Do I think right?"

"Not exactly," said Loptr, and he turned his face away for a moment, then looked back, meeting Boniface's gaze. "I — I know I have always been cold with you. That I have always been... cold. But tonight that won't sustain me, and I have need of someone's warmth. I should like it to be yours, if you will give it."

"Is that a proposition?" asked Boniface, the response automatic, and Loptr pressed his lips together, like he was trying not to smile. "I'm sorry, highness, I'm — A joke. That's all. I'll stay with you, I will."

His majesty didn't join them for dinner — he was buried in paperwork, still working, and so they didn't take their meal in one of the dining halls that Boniface had eaten in before, but in Loptr's bedchambers, into which Boniface had never so much as stepped.

The weren't at all like Fenris', which had a great many furs and hunting trophies thrown over stone and leathers — Loptr favoured comfortable, push furnishings, and the room was carpeted, wallpapered, the sheets made of green silk woven with gold, bookshelves lining every wall.

"No potions lab?" he asked over dinner, and Loptr laughed.

"A very dangerous thing to keep in one's bedchambers," he murmured. "The convenience appeals, but it would be dangerous, I think. I'd want to experiment at all hours, and I'd be liable to set myself alight or poison myself with some accidental vapour."

"I never, um..." Boniface said, and he shook his head.

Across the table, Loptr looked at him thoughtfully, taking a sip of his wine. "You're not... You aren't from magic, are you?"

"Um, no, not — Not active magic," said Boniface, shaking his head. He'd never had this discussion with Loptr before, but nor had he discussed it with Fenris or anybody else in years. People asked him now and then about his life before he came to Einsamal, but it was ordinarily curiosity about magical life when lived close to mundies, or questions about his family, his ancestors.

No one really asked about his childhood, and he didn't tend to volunteer the information, knew that it was... Well, suffice it to say, it wasn't the sort of anecdote people really wanted, wasn't what they wanted to hear. It wasn't as though Einsamal existed in complete isolation, but there was a separation, an intentional one, from magical human socicties, and while Virtue was an exception to that rule, it was not because Virtue's humans were considered all that much more palatable than the rest.

It was an old political decision, made because of treaties Virtue had with nearby fae kingdoms, made respectable by extension.

"I was born and raised in Virtue," said Boniface. "My father is the Head of the Treasury, but my family have a, um... You never looked it up, did you? You didn't think of me as a dignitary, or anything like that."

"To be entirely honest with you," said Loptr in an even, modulated voice, "I am not in favour of the Virtue exchange. My mother was vehemently opposed to it, and although she used to counsel my father against it... Well, suffice it to say, when came your drawing from the lottery, and Kari Astridson's, Mother was already on her deathbed, and in no fit state to bring her case to the Einsamal Court. I intend to do so myself before comes the next draw."

"Is that why you always hated me?"

"I don't hate you," said Loptr seriously. "I've never hated you. I am simply... a man attached to my solitude, and more than that, it's never sat well with me that we took you from your family and dispatched a young girl from hers. This exchange we have, as far as I see it, it's... archaic. There are those of Virtue who would come to Einsamal willingly, as adults, as — as tourists.

"It was my mother's vision that we might foster a mutual exchange of adults who simply desire to travel, as is more customary between modern nation-states. I look at you, Boniface, and I see a man stranded on an island not his own. You command no great magic of your own, and you have been taught skills that are centuries departed from the man you would have been — skills of a tradition to which you have no tie but random chance and a political custom for which there is no longer any call.

"It made you very ill to come here, and would make you very ill to leave — you can't even sail the islands after decades with us. We have trapped you here, and there is no reason to think you might have come here of your own volition. You were robbed of an informed decision."

Boniface stared down at the tabletop, and Loptr exhaled.

"I'm sorry," he said. "I don't say this to shame you, merely — I regret that you were made to come here. That no choice was really allotted you."

"If it's any consolation," said Boniface, not knowing what to make of his own emotions, "I'm very glad to be here. I'd do it again, if given the choice — I'm happier here than I could ever imagine, going back to Virtue. Einsamal is my home, your highness. If I wanted to leave, I would have by now."

Loptr's nostrils flared, and Boniface didn't know what to make of his distant expression as he gave a neat bow of his head.

"I'm sorry," he said again. "I didn't let you tell me about your family, I... I don't know anything about them, no."

"My father is Head of the Treasury in Virtue," said Boniface slowly. "My grandfather served in the government for all of his life, as well, um... My great-grandfather was Prime Minister between 1966 and 1972."

Loptr was staring at him, his lips parted, and Boniface smiled.

"Yeah," he said. "And, um, my mother is a surgeon. A cardiothoracic surgeon — heat surgery, lung surgery, oesophageal surgeries... Anything up here." He gestured to his chest, and Loptr nodded his head. "Every school in Virtue is magical fusion. When I was a kid, I did study enchantment, I got taught the basics, but I never had any skill with active magic. I am sensitive to it, though, I feel it when we move around the island, and I can feel when something's enchanted."

Loptr was looking at him seriously over his food as they ate, and he seemed to hesitate before he asked, "Do you — Do you regret receiving no magical tutelage? Is that something you wished we might have given you?"

"No," said Boniface, laughing, and he shook his head. "No, I don't think so — and it's not like no one ever taught me anything, not like I couldn't have asked Is, or asked your father to refer me to someone. I've learned how to use enchanted weapons, how to wield them, how to use enchanted tools. My rapier's got enchantments in it, and I'm not an apothecary like you are, but I can brew a lot of basic healing stuff in the field, a lot of magical first aid. I can use my fucking, um... Is taught me how to quick enchant pieces of metal to make a defibrillator in the field, so I know how to do that."

"Would you like to learn more, though?" asked Loptr, tilting his head. "Knowing what you do thus far, would you desire to command magic as I do, as Is does, were it possible for you to learn?"

"I don't know," said Boniface, wondering if there was a correct answer, if there was a particular answer that Loptr was looking for, but if there was, he made no show of being disappointed with the answer he gave. "I... Your highness, you must understand that already, the life I live here, it's something out of a storybook. If I were in Virtue, living the life I've lived thus far — Well, for one, I'd be at least twice the age I am, not still looking as young as I do, and I'd probably be like my father, I'd be a civil servant. Filing papers, pursuing... governmental bureaucracy. Look at me: I wear leathers and I carry a sword and I kill monsters and I serve the princes of a magical island. That's — I know that it's your life, that it's natural to you, normal, but to me? This *is* magic. I've been very lucky. I'm very grateful."

"No regrets?"

"No regr— Your highness, the only regret I've ever had, living here as I do, is in my failure to befriend you as I have your brother. To gain your approval, your affection, as I have his."

Loptr looked genuinely unhappy with that, and Boniface felt his chest ache, not knowing what to say to soothe him, to fix it. This was a night out of his fantasies, the two of them sat down to dinner together, and yet none of the things he'd previously rehearsed in his head — love songs, poetry, declarations of affection, requests for favour — came to his tongue. It was too real, too simple, too... Normal.

It was surreal.

"I didn't know why," said Boniface quietly. "I didn't know that you regretted that I came here the way that I did. I just thought it was... me."

"I wouldn't simplify things to that extent," said Loptr. "To think my coldness toward you is borne only of your circumstances here is... too forgiving. To me, of my flaws."

"You have no flaws," said Boniface, and Loptr huffed out an irritated sound that was also a laugh, no matter that he tried to hide it.

"Don't do that," he murmured. "You make yourself very easy to dislike, when you do that."

"When I flirt?"

"When you lie, and lie the way that you do — obviously, and blatantly, with no attempt made to pretend that's not what you're doing."

"I see a beautiful face, I jump to flattery," said Boniface, shrugging his shoulders. "It's the instinct at the core of my being, your highness." He took up his wine and drank from the glass, and when Loptr didn't say anything, said, "I — You are beautiful. You've never let me tell you before, but I've desired you since first I laid eyes on you."

"Yes," said Loptr. "Yes, I... I know."

It was Boniface's turn to stare now, and to Loptr's credit there seemed to be real regret in his face as he looked into the depths of his wine glass and then across at Boniface again, his lips twisting as he seemed to carefully consider what it was he was about to say.

"I've never spoken to you of the magic I use," he said. "What has my brother said?"

"That you're a powerful mage," said Boniface slowly. "One of the most powerful in Einsamal."

"Mmm, anyone on the island could tell you that — and they'd tell you for the sheer propagandic value, whether it was true or not." Boniface's lips twitched, and he pressed them together to keep from laughing out loud. "What has he, or anyone else, told you of my actual ability? Concrete things, not just vague words about the power I might wield?"

"Um, I know you channel power to the gods," said Boniface slowly. "Or — Whatever the fuck, the ritual stuff you do every year, that stuff.

You can command the elements, you can do some basic healing, some fleshturning — you can knit together broken bones, so long as it's a clean break, and heal arterial cuts, so long as you can see what you're doing. He said you once gave yourself gills to breathe underwater."

"A mistake that was," Loptr murmured, "and not one I'd repeat. Some nights I still wake up coughing water."

Boniface chuckled, trying to imagine that — Loptr always seemed an image of perfection, never so much as getting cut or injured, let alone fucking up one of his spells. It was difficult to envision him messing up something as crucial as breathing.

"I have a future-sight," said Loptr. "Everything I see, Boniface, I see in layers of meaning and reality — past, present, future. I see echoes of it all as though seeing several pages of a book all at once. I see a boy, and at once I see who he is, the young man he will become, and the wizened old fellow he will become after that, if he should be so lucky; I see scars before they are even wounds; I look at the sky outside, and I see it in every shade at once, I see it peaceful and I see it roiling."

"When it storms, you sneeze," said Boniface, at a loss as to what else to say.

"That's true," said Loptr evenly. "Although that doesn't really have anything to do with my divinatory capacity. It's just that the latent magics of this island tickle my nose when storm clouds roll in. Some people sneeze in sunlight."

"I do," said Boniface softly.

"Yes," said Loptr, his lips shifting into a small smile, and it seemed to him that there was affection in it, or so he hoped.

"It's called a photic sneeze reflex," said Boniface. "I used to get it more at home — not because of the sun, that's the same, but bright lights, inside, they'd give me a tickle in my nose. That doesn't happen here. Candlelight is softer, easier on the eye. Is there — You're telling me this for a reason."

"I have always struggled to make friends, connections," said Loptr. "Fenris is my brother, and I love him dearly, desperately, as is my duty. As was my duty to my mother. It's not an excuse, as I tell you this, that I have difficulties accustoming to other people's presences, their... pasts, futures, presents. Merely an — an explanation. The precursor to my apology for the cruelty with which I have treated you, these decades between us, the distance I've fostered and forced between us. My cold heart, my biting words. I am sorry, Boniface."

"You want my forgiveness, highness, you have it," he said immediately.

"I don't, actually," said Loptr. "I don't think you should forgive me."

"A shame it's not your choice then," said Boniface, giving the prince a small smile.

Loptr stared at him for some moments, and when he returned the smile it was slow and had a reservation in it, one Boniface couldn't exactly put his finger on. He wanted to ask, ached to ask, but here was the tenuous beginning of what seemed like it might be an actual friendship with the man, and the very idea of hurting it, shattering that beginning—

He didn't think he could bear to do that.

"Do you think I sing well?" asked Boniface.

"You sing passably," said Loptr. "I wouldn't have you sing less, but I wouldn't have you sing more, either."

"You wound me, your highness."

Loptr chuckled, pouring more wine. That reservation, that strange sense of distance, lingered in his eyes and the set of his mouth for the whole of the evening.

* * *

Boniface left in the early hours of the morning, escorted by a member of the guard back to his own lodgings outside of the palace proper, and Loptr slept fitfully, only able to sleep at all because of the strength of the alcohol he'd been imbibing the night through.

He didn't leave his bed come morning, and declined lunch when he was called to it.

It was early evening when Fenris came into his quarters without even knocking, as was his wont, with a tray of bread, cheese, and fruit balanced on one arm.

Loptr didn't stir from where he was buried under his blankets, his face mashed into his pillows, as he watched his brother move into the room, setting the tray on the side table and pouring Loptr water when he found his glass was empty.

"You're awake," he said.

"I am," said Loptr.

"You're ill?"

"No," said Loptr. "Merely tired, that's all."

"Boniface said he accompanied you riding yesterday," said Fenris, and Loptr felt his blood turn cold, but as Fenris pulled back the blankets and climbed into the bed beside him, throwing his legs ridiculously over Loptr's in a way that was intended to make him laugh, and ordinarily would have, he followed it up with, "said you were gathering potions ingredients?"

"Mm," Loptr hummed in vague assent, and let out a low *"oof"* as Fenris withdrew his legs and commenced to lie entirely on top of him, his elbow digging between Loptr's shoulders until Loptr rolled from beneath him, kicking his brother.

Fenris dropped forward, lying on his belly as Loptr was, resting in parallel to him.

"What ails you?" he asked quietly. "I met Boniface this morning, and he was brimming over with your praises, said again and again how happy he was to have finally pleased you in some way, to be afforded your friendship. Has speaking to one man over dinner so exhausted you? So extinguished the light within?"

"I'm no friend of Boniface's," murmured Loptr, resting his chin on his forearms. "You're his friend — you, Lux, Umbra, Frum. All those young men and women he entices into his bed, or entices into allowing into their beds. All those people he sings songs to and writes poetry for, they're his friends. I am no one's friend, Fenris. I am a child of Loki, as is my lot in life — Oath-Breaker, Betrayer, Bound By Circumstance."

"What the fuck are you talking about?" asked Fenris, and Loptr just shook his head, not able to say it, not able to explain.

How could he?

For all Fenris knew, he had fought off the weight of his mother's curse with the meditative techniques Loptr's mother had taught him, and that was the end of it. Why should he no anything else?

Fenris leaned in closer, putting his cheek against Loptr's shoulder, and Loptr responded in kind, resting his head on top of Fenris', his chin resting in his brother's hair.

"He said you regretted his coming from Virtue," said Fenris. "Said you would end the exchange."

"I would," said Loptr. "I've told you that before."

"You have," Fenris allowed, "but you've never told him that. Never given him any reason for keeping him at arm's length — I assumed, as with most everything else, you kept him away because you don't like your solitude being interrupted. Something was different, yesterday."

"Something," said Loptr. "Nothing particularly, just... A man does tire of solitude, you know."

"I know," said Fenris, his voice as soft as he could get it, his cheek warm on Loptr's shoulder, his beard quite horrible, but it hardly seemed the time to complain. "I didn't expect you to ever admit it, least of all to Boniface."

"I admitted nothing to him that wasn't true," said Loptr. "Do you love him?"

"Boniface? Of course, he's a good friend, a brother of mine — a brother of yours too. I love him just as dearly as I do the twins and Frum. I've trusted him with my life, and would again. You wouldn't?"

Loptr was quiet for a few moments, feeling the thickness of Fenris' hair under his chin, smelling the fragrance from his soap. He considered what it might be like to try to fight Fenris off him, off of Father, were he buried in the throes of Odin's cursed madness, see the back of him as he disappeared into the mists, or see his corpse bloodied and dead-eyed on the floor.

"I would," said Loptr quietly. "I've always known I could trust him, even from the beginning, he's— For the world he comes from, he's fearless, carries his courage in his breast."

"I've never known you to speak so positively about him," murmured Fenris, sounding pleased. "Did Boniface do something to please you he was too modest to tell me?"

Loptr forced a laugh, knowing that Fenris couldn't see his face, and he dropped his head back down to the mattress, groaned a complaint when Fenris responded by flopping on top of him, using his back as a pillow and picking up Loptr's book, but he didn't struggle free, just relaxed with the other man's weight on top of him.

Fenris didn't say anything, just lingered until Loptr finally sat up and ate half of what was on the tray, and then he kissed Loptr's forehead and left him be. Once he was gone, Loptr stared around at the room, at the echo of Boniface sitting at his dining table, one that he'd never noticed there before, never particularly made out even though he ought have, in between those of Fenris and Father and Mother.

It had felt unreal, leading Boniface into his quarters, gesturing for him to sit, and yet real it was, Boniface there, Boniface solid and real and complete in his entirety, in his warm smiles and his eyes, wide as they were, such a deep and soulful brown.

"Is no one ever beside you when you look at your reflection, Loptr?"

How many times had his mother asked him that, one time or another? It had been a great concern of hers in the last of her dying days, in that last year or so where she was asleep more hours than she was awake, where she was always hazy and somewhat confused. A great many times she'd asked him — more times than he could count.

He'd always brushed her off, always refused to answer, had been playful, had feigned ignorance, had given an answer that was no real answer at all, and either way, she'd forget it soon after.

Loptr stood in front of the mirror now and saw the echo of Boniface at his shoulder, his lips smiling, up on his tiptoes so he could rest his chin on the upper part of Loptr's forearm, sparks showing golden in his brown eyes. He was there and not there at once, an echo of what could be and what wasn't at once — there were futures that were certain, and futures that blinked in and out of potential. The latter ones were the cruellest — he'd used to see his mother standing on her feet about the place, sometimes, even knowing her recovery was beyond the realms of real possibility *unless* he...

And that was it, wasn't it?

Loki called it his madness, and a madness it was, a curse as much Fenris' curse was — futures that he could have, that he could reach for so easily, taunted him. His mother *could* have been healed, had he only done the unthinkable — had he resorted to the slaughter of a man or two, and channelled the product of that slaughter, he might have used that energy to heal her in her entirety. He might be as powerful as his visions occasionally saw fit to reflect him as, if he only he did what he would not do — if he petitioned the gods and bargained for it, if he stole it, if he murdered for it.

He'd always suspected that Boniface was the same.

For once, he'd thought it was something almost mundane, something simple — he'd thought it was that Boniface was a human boy of no prospects. How stupid had he been, to think it was something as simple as that, to think it was merely Boniface's station that should prevent Loptr from drawing him near?

He was a prince in his own right, as far as Virtue could be seen to have an equivalent of the thing, and Loptr hardly had to fear trapping him in Einsamal, because by his own admission he was grateful to have come here.

There was nothing stopping that echo from being real and solid and warm and complete except for the fact that Loptr could only have it if he traded his sanity or his brother for it.

Loptr stared at his reflection in the mirror, saw the shimmer of the tears on his cheeks before they were real and touched his fingers to his face where it was as-yet dry. Sighing, he closed his eyes and turned away from the mirror before his cheeks could become wet.

* * *

"Will you ride with me again?" asked Loptr, and Boniface looked up from where he was sitting on a bench in the medicinal gardens, enjoying the sun on his face as he polished his rapier, felt the blade smooth and clean and shimmering under the cloth. Funny — walking these days, he felt naked without the familiar weight of it at his hip, like it was part of him, an extension of him.

"To the same place?" asked Boniface. "To the same... danger?"

"To the same place," said Loptr. "But I wanted to show you this time, it's, ah... Long ago, that stone building, the cavern carved beneath it, it was an arena not dissimilar to the one we have here in the palace grounds, although it is somewhat larger. Years ago I began cultivating a garden there, and I have, ah... I've neglected it in recent years."

"A garden?" Boniface repeated, and he felt his lips smile.

"It's nothing like this one," said Loptr, gesturing to the pots of blooming flowers, the great many herbs and bushes growing. "The magic is thick there, old. It was there I took my lessons when I was a small boy, when first I learned to channel what power I have, and I was taught to... to heal, to command elements, to channel latent magic on the air and spin it as I needed. My mother would play with me there, before she became ill."

His voice was quiet and had a softness to it, his hands clasped in front of his belly, and Boniface nodded his head, getting to his feet and buckling his scabbard around his waist.

"Your mother was a wonderful woman," said Boniface as he walked with Loptr down the winding steps to the gates, their elbows brushing against each other as they walked in parallel to one another. "I was always struck by how kind she was, even on the nights where she was confused or disoriented, always so gentle."

Loptr hummed, nodding his head. He wasn't dressed to ride, wasn't wearing the breeches he'd worn the other day, and as his robes moved back and forth, the skirt swaying on the steps beneath them, it sometimes brushed against Boniface's ankles, his calves. He'd dressed in tunics before, although it wasn't his preference, but he'd never worn robes like that even when messing about and dressing up — he couldn't help but wonder what it was like, if Loptr was calmed by it or comforted by it, the weight of the skirts, the way the fabric layered but was so loose.

"What— What was wrong with her? Exactly?"

"She contracted a particularly hardy strain of what we commonly call Dryad's Influenza when she was only a young woman," said Loptr. "She dealt with complications from it for most of her life, mostly strain on her lungs and her heart which she kept in check with several prescribed medications, but further wear was unfortunately inevitable. Her heartbeats became irregular, and increasingly when she breathed, she wasn't getting enough oxygen — there was then further strain on her other organs, her brain, her liver. She was not in any real pain, which was a relief, but it was slow, and that slow pace was painful for me, nursing her through it knowing there was no end in sight except death."

"Is it common? Dryad's Influenza?"

"No, not particularly," was Loptr's simple answer. "There was a vaccine program amongst wood nymphs across Europe a century or so ago, amongst whom the worst of the strains developed and evolved.

It's very rarely seen now. Mother was a significant contributor to that program's development."

Boniface took this in, thinking about Queen Ingrid weak and exhausted in her bed, looking so much older than King Leon ever did, although they were apparently the same age. "She was part nymph?"

"On her mother's side. You're entirely human, aren't you?"

Boniface looked at him, leaning to try to get a look at his face, not sure if it was a joke or not. "Well," he said. "I mean, not anymore. If I was still human, you know, I'd be... Well. I'll live as long as you guys will, if I stay here. I heal from unthinkable wounds, my stamina, my strength, it's all different here. I don't channel magic like you do, don't cast spells, but magic runs through me now. That doesn't happen without wreaking changes on someone."

"Of course," said Loptr, as though he'd forgotten — maybe he had forgotten. "I'm sorry, I never thought about that. Never considered it. Does it — Does that stop you from leaving Einsamal? Make you hesitate to visit your family?"

"I don't really want to visit my family," Boniface admitted. "I write them letters, and they write me back, but, uh... It's not as if I wouldn't see them if they came here, you know. But I went to a boarding school and I never saw them that much anyway."

"And your grandfather? He was a politician too, you said."

"Yeah, but he died when I was five, I think. All my grandparents were dead by the time I was twelve — it was just my parents I left behind when I came here. Astrid and Amund, they've always been good to me — and Prince Fenris, King Leon. I don't know. Perhaps it's callous to say, but I feel I have more family here than I did back there."

"And marriage?"

"Marriage?" repeated Boniface, and he laughed, shaking his head.

"How many beautiful women have you spent the night with, this past year?"

"Oh, I don't know," muttered Boniface.

"How many nights with handsome men?"

"Not as many as I have with beautiful women."

"But quite a few?"

"A fair few, yes, highness. Is that against the law?"

"It's against no law," said Loptr. "I merely wonder that you wouldn't marry any of them, given the chance. Do you not desire for that? Marriage, children?"

"Of course," said Boniface immediately, and for some reason his cheeks felt somewhat warm at the way Loptr was looking at him, loose locks of his hair framing the beauty of his face as he leaned forward to better see Boniface's expression, to listen to him all the more intently. "I would marry, yes, and I'd like children, too, a few of them. But when a rakish bard plays a lute and improvises poetry about the colour of your hair and the taste of your lips in a busy tavern, you don't look down at him and think of him as ideal material, as far as husbands go. You think of him as good for a night, for two nights — good for a meal and a pleasant time, good for how he makes you feel, how he soothes your woes, warms your heart. How he makes your thighs tremble."

"A pleasant time, soothed woes, a warm heart, trembling thighs," repeated Loptr, and he laughed quietly. "Perhaps I'm simply not as well-seasoned as the people you bed, but these all seem like worthy qualities in a spouse to me."

"Marry me, then," said Boniface.

Loptr was suddenly still on the path, and Boniface felt his breath hitch in his throat. "Your highness—"

And then Loptr's mouth was on his, and for all the coolness of his hands as they cupped Boniface's cheeks, his lips were warm and they tingled with magic and electricity, made Boniface thrum from the inside. Boniface kissed him back, put one hand on Loptr's waist and the other on the side of his neck — he had to tilt back his head to allow for it, what with the height difference between them, but it was more than worth it, was quite wonderful.

Loptr broke apart from him, and Boniface stared into his eyes, marvelled at the shining pale brown of one eye, the colour of ale, and the marvellous green of the other.

"You know," he said breathlessly, "your highness, your eyes—"

"Oh, please, Boniface," Loptr interrupted him, his expression oddly stern. "No poetry, I couldn't bear it."

"Your highness," he said, and Loptr touched his chin, pressed his thumb against the hair there, dragging his nail over Boniface's goatee. It tickled, made him laugh, and he reached up, sliding his palm around Loptr's wrist, his thumb against the point of his pulse.

"It's mad that you call Fenris highness," said Loptr quietly. "You don't need to, you know. You can call him by his name — and me by mine."

"Prince—"

"Mm," hummed Loptr, squeezing slightly, and Boniface exhaled.

"Loptr," he whispered, and on his tongue the word tasted like a prayer. "Shall we ride, then?"

"Please," said Loptr, gesturing ahead of them. "Lead the way."

* * *

Sitting on the floor of the clearing, his back to one of the stone pillars, Loptr put his head in his hands, his fingers gripping tightly at his hair, and he sobbed. Each sound was ragged, painful, pulling at his throat, his lungs, at the very core of him, his cheeks wet with it as above him, the skies began their slow turn from blue to peachy reds, threatening the inky black that would come.

He couldn't stop crying, and didn't bother to try.

* * *

The arena was a great, cavernous room, lit from a rounded skylight, and Boniface felt his lips part as he moved slowly down the stairs to the garden Loptr had mentioned. He was right — it was overgrown, all thick grasses and meadow flowers with ivy-messy pots around the outside, and he felt himself smile as he went quickly down them.

"Loptr?" he asked, calling back when he didn't hear the other man behind him, but he didn't see him either. He stopped on the step, scanning the stairs and the hallway for him, then glancing around the rest of the room, but there was no sign of him. Loptr had been right behind him — had he stayed outside after all?

"Leave Loptr for now," said a voice from the centre of the garden, and Boniface jumped nearly out of his skin, turning to look at him.

He was tall, had a mane of red hair and different coloured eyes, one grey and one green, and Boniface immediately moved back from him so fast that he stumbled and landed on his arse on the steps.

"Yes," said Loki softly. "You know who I am, don't you?"

"Lord L— Lord," said Boniface, half-turning to scramble up the steps, "I'm sorry, I didn't—"

"Stop," said Lord Loki. "Stay precisely where you are."

Boniface's hands froze on the stone, and he realised he was breathing heavy, his heart beginning to pound faster in his chest.

"I made your prince a bargain, Boniface," said Lord Loki, and Boniface couldn't stand to look at his face directly, at the sparks and fire around his eyes, his hair. "His brother is unwell — did you know that?"

"No, lord," whispered Boniface.

"You wouldn't know, of course," said Lord Loki, and his lips were smirking when Boniface risked a glance at them, but didn't risk looking up at his eyes. "Prince Loptr has staved off his brother's illness, taken on the burden for himself — and like a cat, hm, he hides his symptoms, would crawl away like such an animal to die before he showed his weakness publicly."

Boniface sat forward, and although he didn't dare to look up at the god, knew that wasn't for the likes of him, he listened intently, his lips pressed tightly together. He glanced once more up toward the entrance, but Loptr was still nowhere to be seen.

"Oh," said Boniface, swallowing. "I did not — I didn't know, lord. Is there anything I can do?"

Loki's laugh was soft, but for all its quiet volume it filled the arena like the thunder of a crowd, and Boniface felt it through his chest, felt it in his very bones. "What can you do?" he asked. "What *would* you do?"

"Anything," said Boniface immediately, leaning forward, his hands on his own knees. "I'll do anything, milord, anything you — anything you want of me, anything you ask."

"For which of them?"

"... Lord?"

"For Fenris or for Loptr — for whom will you do *anything*?"

"Either," said Boniface. "Both."

"Prince Loptr came to this place two days ago," said Loki softly. He was moving forward, and Boniface stared at his feet as they moved through the grass, his steps slow and soft and silent. The closer he got, the thicker the crackle on the air felt, sparking and thick in his ears, slick on his tongue, between his teeth. "He, too, said he would do anything to save his brother and himself, to ensure this sickness was staved off once and for all. I named my price."

Boniface was silent, not understanding, his brow furrowing, as he stared at Loki's shoes.

They were basketball shoes, white-laced and white-soled. They didn't exactly match his mage's robes.

"I told him I would heal his ills," said Lord Loki, "and heal his brother's too. And do you know what I asked in return?"

"No, lord."

"You."

Boniface stared at Loki's shoes, and then no matter that it hurt his eyes, no matter that it made them sting, he tipped back his head and he looked up at Lord Loki's face, at the slight smirk pulling at his lips, the glitter in his mismatched eyes. He didn't care that Loptr's heterochromia made him a *child of Loki* — the two of them looked nothing alike, and even the green of their green eyes was different, one wholly unlike the other.

"M— Me?" he asked. There was a cold, sinking feeling in his chest, and he felt nauseated and unwell as he bowed his head forward. It somewhat recontextualised the past few days — Loptr's grief and apparent unease as he'd come from the temple, his sudden warmth and friendliness toward Boniface these past few days.

The kiss.

The *kiss*, Loptr's mouth on his, his lips sweet and wonderful and oh-so-warm, his hands so cool—

A farewell kiss, then. An apology, perhaps.

"V— Very well, my lord," whispered Boniface. "What— What now?"

"What now?"

"You named your price, lord, and that was me. His highness has me delivered — that's price paid. So what do I do?"

"Perhaps you don't do anything," said Loki. "Perhaps you die, here and now — perhaps I kill you where you lie, and eat your heart as it yet beats."

Boniface's blood was cold in his veins, and he closed his eyes tightly, thought about Loptr's lips on his, his cold wit, his books and his studies — he thought about Fenris, Fenris' booming laugh, his bright eyes, his strength, his jokes.

"Ought I remove my— Strip off my armour, lord? To ease your way?"

Loki started laughing, and Boniface shuddered at the sound it made, crackling unnaturally on the air in a way more like real thunder than like a normal sound — it pounded in his ears, through his chest, and he didn't want to look up, didn't want to feel his eyes ache again, but he sat in his place anticipant of the killing blow.

"What say you, boy, I make you a bargain?"

"Do I have the power to bargain with you, lord? If I'm— if I've been given over to you?"

"Good question," said Loki. "Yes, boy, since I see fit to give it to you. Here are my terms: you walk back up those stairs, and you go out of that archway... And at some point, when I see fit to demand it of you, you will do me a favour."

"A favour?"

"A favour. I will ask you to do some act for me."

"That's— That's it?"

"That's it."

Boniface's breath hitched as he inhaled, and he asked slowly, "What act? To— To harm someone, hurt... someone?"

"You don't get to ask what the favour will be," said Loki softly. "You don't get to place restrictions on it. You live now, and agree to these terms, or you die."

It was not the most enticing of offers, and carried with it its own risk, but he should rather live than die — and Loptr, surely, would rather... He liked to think, in any case. He *would* like to think. "And I can go right now? I don't... You won't eat my heart?"

"Your prince had the power to betray you to me," said Loki softly. "To hand you over to me. Something tells me your heart was beyond his power to give."

"It's no betrayal," said Boniface immediately. "I'm loyal to the Prince Fenris and Loptr both — I'd give my life for either of them. They know that, Loptr knows that."

"Hm," said Loki. "You'll take my terms, then? Go free, and know you owe a favour?"

"Yes," whispered Boniface. "Yes, please, yes— Thank you."

"Then go," said Loki. "Before I change my mind."

Boniface couldn't scramble fast enough up the stairs again.

* * *

"Your highness?" came Boniface's voice beside him, and Loptr jumped in his place, then shot to his feet. Boniface let out a sound of surprise when Loptr's hands came to cup his cheeks, his thumbs sliding under Boniface's eyes before he cupped under his chin, put his hand in Boniface's hair and another on his chest, slid both palms down to his hips, his waist, his thighs, then grabbed his arms, his wrists, examined his hands.

He couldn't control his breathing, knew that his breaths were running fast and shallow, and Boniface stared up at him, his lips parting, before he reached out and touched Loptr back, his cheek.

"Loptr," he said softly. "You've been crying."

"I didn't think you were coming back out," Loptr admitted, his lips pressing together as he did his best not to sniffle, not to further cry, although he was aware of the wetness on his cheeks, the dryness about his eyes, the thickness in his nose, his throat. "Oh, I'm so — I'm so very sorry, but it was..."

Boniface's expression was blank, not comprehending, and Loptr watched his face as he glanced back behind him to the stone archway, the shadow beyond, inside. He studied Boniface's expression, the slight furrow of his brow, the barest tilt of his head.

"I... did go in there, didn't I?" he asked softly, and Loptr stared at his eyes, saw the distance in them, the focus as Boniface looked inwards, wracked his brains for some memory he could not grasp hold of. "Your garden, I saw your garden. The grass, the flowers. I made an agreement with..." He trailed off, stumbled on his words. Looked confused, and made uncertain by that confusion.

"To what terms did you agree?" asked Loptr lowly, his voice more urgent than he meant to allow it to be.

"I — I'm sorry, highness. I really don't know." He bit his lip, and his palm was so soft against Loptr's cheek, softer and warmer than he ever would have let himself imagine, would have let himself dream of. "You've been crying, what's wrong?"

Loptr opened his mouth, thought to explain, to describe it all — and where should he start? With his mother's illness, her death? With the madness allotted Fenris? The madness allotted Loptr? His betrayal of Boniface, his offering of Boniface to Loki to save himself and his brother, because he so little valued Boniface himself?

Here he had been sitting, sobbing, aching with each wretched gasp and choke, thinking of how to explain it to Fenris, to his friends, to his father, and here—

Here Boniface was.

He had bargained his way out of this, agreeing to what terms Loptr had no way of divining, and his memory was blank, made fuzzy and uncertain in that way of the gods. Where was Loptr to start in his explanations? *I betrayed you? I sacrificed you? I have never let myself love you, and thinking you would soon be gone, I've faltered in that resistance?*

"I hate to see you cry," murmured Boniface. "I'd shake worlds to see your smile, but this? What can I do, highness, to make it stop?"

"Call me Loptr," he said.

"Very well," replied Boniface, and smiled at him. "Loptr."

Whatever agreement he had made, it could well be dangerous — likely was, likely *would* be dangerous. He was cupping a ticking timebomb in his palms, made dangerous by a god himself, and yet it was Boniface — Boniface, who adored him.

Boniface, whose lips were soft beneath his, yielded so entirely to Loptr's mouth and then kissed him fiercely, stood up on his tiptoes to allow himself the leverage, and Loptr, weak, so tired of being cold and strong and aloof, kissed him back.

* * *

For such a small man, Boniface sprawled in Loptr's bed, and when Loptr stood to take in some of the night air, left him slumbering underneath Loptr's sheets with his face mashed into Loptr's pillow and the marks of Loptr's mouth marking his body, he couldn't help his smiling lips, the way they curved without his permission.

Fenris had already shot him a knowing look at dinner, arched his eyebrows and mercifully, said nothing.

It was not Fenris who awaited him, sitting on the balcony wall with mundie shoes upon his feet, kicking them playfully against the air.

"You gave him back," he whispered.

"We came to an agreement," said Loki, shrugging his shoulders.

"On what terms?" asked Loptr, and Loki met his gaze, his eyes sparking as he softly laughed.

"You know," he murmured, tapping a finger against his lips, "I really don't recall. I suppose we'll find out when it comes down to it. I can still take him from you, boy, if it suits me to do so."

"Don't," whispered Loptr. "Please, my lord, don't."

"We shall see, child, if he earns his place here," said Loki quietly, his smile as cold as ice, and as Loptr moved forward he evaporated to naught, just fog dissipating into the evening air.

Loptr put his palms on the balcony wall, looking out over Einsamal below.

For all his dread threatened to choke him, it faltered when Boniface stumbled onto the balcony with one of Loptr's robes wrapped around his body, swimming in the fabric, the skirt trailing on the ground.

"Loptr, please," he complained. "Don't you know I'm freezing in that bed of yours?"

"Here, come," murmured Loptr, and drew Boniface close to him, feeling a strange, possessive thrill at the sight of his robes on Boniface's shoulders. "Freeze out here with me instead."

Boniface laughed, and Loptr captured his mouth, swallowed that mirth for his own.

He could stave off thoughts of whatever new curse he'd acquired for himself when the two of them parted ways.

FIN.

More from the Author

If you'd like to seek out more of my work, *Heart of Stone* is a full-length novel set in the 18th century, and is a slowburn slice-of-life romance between a vampire and his secretary, the vampire ADHD and the secretary autistic. It has a lot of humour and domestic elements throughout.

My most recent release, *Powder and Feathers*, is a long-form contemporary dark romance with a great many fantasy elements, featuring a fucked-up dynamic between a Fallen angel and a depressed artist he begins stalking in the park.

If you're interested in perusing more novella-length pieces and short stories, I publish a huge variety of short stories that are available on a subscription model from Patreon[1] or as part of your Medium[2] subscription!

I normally publish at least one new piece a week, whether that's short stories, longer form short stories like this one, serial updates for my chaptered works, or non-fiction pieces like essays and analyses.

My name is Johannes T. Evans on both sites.

My website: www.JohannesTEvans.com[3]

My Twitter: @JohannesTEvans[4]

And finally, if you'd like to get regular email updates from me, with media recommendations, links to my most recently published work, and other little announcements, you can sign up at www.buttondown.email/ JohannesTEvans.

---

1.   https://www.patreon.com/JohannesEvans

2.   https://johannestevans.medium.com/directory-of-work-6291c6e102b9

3.   http://www.JohannesTEvans.com

4.   https://twitter.com/johannestevans